Susan Thompson

THE MUSEUM OF ODDITIES

A Two-Wheeled Detective Mystery

Susan Thompson spent twenty years in the adult literacy field as a teacher, program director, curriculum developer, trainer, and mentor to adult literacy professionals. She is a graduate of Hollins University, the New School Certificate Program in adult literacy, and a recipient of the 2011 Literacy Recognition Award from the New York City Literacy Assistance Center. A lifelong reader of mystery stories, Susan lives in Brooklyn, New York.

First published by Gemma in 2023.

www.gemmamedia.org

Printed in the United States of America

978-1-956476-27-9

Library of Congress Cataloging-in Publication Data available.

Cover by Laura Shaw Design

Named after the brightest star in the Northern Crown, Gemma is a nonprofit organization that helps new readers acquire English language literacy skills with relevant, engaging books, eBooks, and audiobooks. Always original, never adapted, these stories introduce adults and young adults to the life-changing power of reading.

Open Door

Cabinets of Curiosity, or **Wonder Rooms**, exhibited a wide variety of objects. They featured examples of natural history (such as stuffed animals, dried insects, and fossils), exotic plants and animals, scientific instruments, and objects created by or modified by humans, like works of art. [Adapted from Google Arts & Culture]

CONTENTS

CAST OF CHARACTERS

Tami Tripper—A professional temporary employee and free spirit.

Raven Moore—Curator. Head of the Museum of Oddities.

Helga Fitzroy—Conservator. Repairs, cleans, and preserves the collection.

Nathan Amos—Archivist. Maintains the computer catalogue.

Willow—Exhibit designer.

Hector Diaz—Head of security.

Selma Simpson—Museum visitor.

A FEW OF THE MANY GALLERIES
IN THE MUSEUM OF ODDITIES

Taxidermy

Carnival Curiosities

Tick Tock

Musical Miracles

Secrets of the Sea

Gems and Jewels

CHAPTER 1

ENTER AND BE AMAZED

Tami pedaled leisurely along the street. What a beautiful spring day. Perfect for riding her bike, Ruby. Tami was not headed any place in particular. Just biking around town.

"Wait a minute! What is this?"

It was an old stone mansion. A carved blue arch framed the double-doored entrance. Insects, birds, reptiles, and mammals frolicked across in bright colors. Above the arch was a sign.

Welcome to the Museum of Oddities
Enter and Be Amazed

Tami jumped off her bike. She was eager to enter and be amazed. And she was. This was what Tami saw that day:

Twenty-seven stuffed animals.
Three music boxes that were two hundred years old and played tunes.
One huge crystal ball.
A chair with a secret drawer. Inside was a tiny carved dog with a tail that wagged.
Shells from distant oceans.
A two-headed duckling.
And an automated fortune teller.

The Museum of Oddities was crowded with all sorts of curious things. They filled the cabinets and covered the shelves. They dangled from the ceiling. They rose from the floor and stood in corners. Each gallery displayed something Tami had never seen before. She spent three hours roaming through the museum. She had a wonderful time. On her way out, Tami stopped to take a photo of the museum's entrance. The blue color of the arch and the creatures that floated across it looked familiar.

Tami biked home full of excitement. She raced up the stairs to her apartment. Only three cozy rooms. Tall windows looked out on the street below. Shelves held Tami's many books. There was a sofa and a chair and a plant. The walls were painted red, Tami's favorite color.

Tami's mom was an abstract artist. Even when she was dying from cancer, Tami's mom painted. Tami often wondered what inspired her mom's canvases. Now she studied one particular painting. Colorful shapes floated across a blue background. Just like the arch above the museum's entrance. Tami read the title on the back of the painting. It said *Enter and Be Amazed*. A warm feeling flooded Tami's heart. It was a connection to her mom.

CHAPTER 2

SWEETIE PIE

Tami returned again and again to the Museum of Oddities. She fell in love with the adorable two-headed duckling. It was tiny and fluffy and had a sweet expression. Both little heads smiled at Tami. The two-headed duckling was not alive. It was stuffed and displayed under a glass dome in the Taxidermy gallery.

Taxidermy is the art of stuffing dead animals. There were many in the gallery. A deer with a large rack of antlers. A rhino head with a horn. A snarling tiger. Birds hung from the ceiling. An eagle. A hummingbird. A swan. Beavers and raccoons posed in display cabinets along with tiny mice and chipmunks.

Tami heard a voice behind her. "I knew I would find you here. You have been here every day. I thought I should say hi. I'm Hector Diaz. I am head of security for the museum."

"I'm Tami Tripper. I think the Museum of Oddities is wonderful. I can't stay away. Especially from this cute duckling."

"Have you given it a name?"

Tami's dark eyes twinkled. "She is so sweet. I will name her Sweetie Pie."

Hector chuckled. "Hello there, Sweetie Pie."

Tami laughed. "I have another favorite. The automated fortune teller in Carnival Curiosities."

"Zelda was discovered in Europe," said Hector. "She still tells fortunes. Maybe she will tell yours."

"I would love that," said Tami. "Have you worked here long, Mr. Diaz?"

"Call me Hector. I have been here fifteen years. After I retired from the police."

"I wish I could work at the Museum of Oddities."

"Are you looking for work?"

"Yes, I am between temp jobs. I hope to find something soon."

"You don't work full-time?"

Why are people always so surprised? thought Tami. "Full-time jobs don't match my personality," she explained. "I like variety. I like change. I like to meet new people. I like to discover new places. I am a *professional temporary employee*. I have many skills," Tami added with pride.

Hector Diaz laughed again. "There might be work here for a *professional temporary employee*. Are you interested?"

"Yes!"

"Let's talk to Raven Moore, the curator. Raven is head of the museum." Hector glanced up at the ceiling security camera. Then he looked back at Tami. "I test every camera every day. Our cameras are fixed in one position. They only view the center of each gallery, not the corners. I worry about theft."

"You don't have guards?"

"No. The board of directors said maybe next year. It is very frustrating.

We have thousands of small objects here."

"I would not want Sweetie Pie stolen," remarked Tami.

CHAPTER 3

A MUSEUM HELPER

Raven Moore's office was on the top floor of the museum. Glass cabinets displayed pieces from the museum's collection. Exhibition posters decorated the walls. Folders piled up on her desk and on the floor. Two computers sat on a long table. Raven Moore was a busy woman.

"Hi Hector. Who is this?" Raven leaned over her desk to shake Tami's hand.

"It is very nice to meet you, Ms. Moore. My name is Tamina Tripper, but everyone calls me Tami. I would love to work here. I am a professional temp with a variety of skills. Also, I am not fussy about the kind of work I do."

"Tami visits all the galleries. She named the little duckling Sweetie Pie," said Hector.

Raven smiled. "Call me Raven, Tami. You may be just what we need."

"Drop by my office later," said Hector on his way out the door.

Raven offered Tami a job as a museum helper. Tami could not believe her luck. This might be my best temp job ever, she thought. I will not be bored at the Museum of Oddities.

Tami found Hector in a small office next to the lobby. "Raven hired me. I am a museum helper. My first task is to dust the objects in the galleries. I am so excited."

"Slow down, Tami. There are two thousand items."

"And all of them are curious!" replied Tami. "I start tomorrow. And thanks!"

Tami hopped onto her bike, Ruby. Tami's mom gave Tami a bicycle when she was nine years old. Tami named the bike Ruby because it was a bright ruby red. Now she always rode a red bike. And she named all of her bikes Ruby to remember her mom.

As Tami pedaled home on Ruby, she hummed a tune she practiced on her clarinet. She often hummed clari-net tunes while she biked. Humming is practice, thought Tami. So far, Tami was a better hummer than a clarinet player. But I am an optimistic person, thought Tami. One day, my clarinet will sound better than my humming!

CHAPTER 4

ZELDA TELLS FORTUNES

The Museum of Oddities was the former home of Abraham Weatherstaff, a collector of rare and unusual objects. Some objects were enormous. Some were tiny. All were strange. When Mr. Weatherstaff died, his collection became a museum with a special mission: *To educate, amaze, and fascinate the curious.* A job at the Museum of Oddities was Tami's idea of heaven on earth. She was educated, amazed, and fascinated by everything she saw.

Tami's favorite gallery was Carnival Curiosities. Equipment from magic shows and traveling circuses were displayed beneath a colorful tent, including:

An enormous crystal ball.
A case of sacred stones.
Thirty-seven decks of tarot cards. Each with a different design.
A full-size wax figure of Harry Houdini, the world's most famous magician and escape artist.
A vanishing booth.
A saw-the-lady-in-half box.
And Zelda, the automated fortune teller.

Tami was curious about the vanishing booth, a popular magician's trick. The booth was the size and shape of a telephone booth. The magician's assistant stepped into the booth. The magician closed the door. Then, when the door opened, surprise, surprise! The booth was empty. The assistant had vanished!

Tami cracked opened the door of the vanishing booth to take a peek. Suddenly, a very tiny, very old woman toppled out, along with two bulging tote bags.

"Oh my gosh," said Tami. She leaned down to help the old woman stand up.

"Oh thank you, dear. Was I asleep? I needed a nap, and the vanishing booth was nearby." Her wrinkled face peered up at Tami. "Who are you, dear?"

"I'm Tamina Tripper. Who are you?"

"Selma Simpson. Everyone here knows me. You can ask."

I think I will ask, thought Tami.

Selma Simpson was another museum oddity. Layers of clothes enveloped her body. A dress hung to her ankles. Over the dress was a vest. Over the vest was a sweater. Then a knitted shawl. On her thinning gray hair, she wore a baseball cap. She wore hiking boots. No socks.

Tami gathered up Selma's totes. A small box fell out. Selma snatched the box from Tami. "That's private." She shoved the box deep into one of the bags. Then she turned to Tami with a smile.

"Tamina is a lovely name. It means strong. Are you true to your name?"

"I try to be." Tami was touched. Most people did not know what Tamina meant. It was another connection to her mother.

Selma noticed Tami's dust mop. "Do you work here, Tamina?"

"Yes, Raven hired me to dust the galleries and help the staff. I really like it here. The Museum of Oddities fascinates me."

"Even more pieces are stored in the basement where Nathan works. He catalogues the collection. I visit Nathan often. He is my best friend."

Selma tottered around the gallery. She whispered to herself. As Tami dusted, she kept an eye on Selma. I think I should ask Hector about her, thought Tami. Just to be sure.

Tami dusted the inside, top, and sides of the vanishing booth and shut the door. Then she approached Zelda, the automated fortune teller. Zelda was in a glass case. She was made out of plaster. Her body stopped just below her waist. Zelda had long black hair and black eyes. She had ruby-red lips. A fringed shawl draped over her shoulders. A lacy veil covered her hair. Silver chains and crystal beads dangled from her neck. She had a mysterious expression.

"Oooh, let's get our fortunes," said Selma. "Do you have a nickel?"

"Only a nickel?"

"Zelda is over one hundred years old. Back then, a nickel could buy many things. Including your fortune."

Tami had two nickels in her pocket. She gave one to Selma, who inserted it into a slot. Creaking sounds issued from inside the glass case. To Tami's amazement, Zelda's head turned from side to side. She raised one arm. A small card dropped out of a chute into Selma's palm.

Beware of an old memory.

Selma's face paled. She frowned at the card. "Ritzy Fitzy?" she whispered.

"Are you alright?" Tami asked.

"Yes," said Selma slowly.

Tami dropped her nickel into the slot. Zelda's head moved from side to side. She raised her arm. A card dropped out.

Strange events are on the horizon.

"That's odd," said Tami. "Fortune cards usually say *Long life will be yours.* Or *Happy times are ahead.*" Tami turned toward Selma with a smile.

But Selma's eyes were back on Zelda. "Is it my lost memory?" She shook her head in confusion. Then she wandered out of the gallery clutching her bags.

CHAPTER 5

WILLOW LOVES TO TALK

Tami did not know whether to be amused by or concerned about Selma Simpson. She hummed and dusted the saw-the-lady-in-half box.

A voice spoke. "If you get inside the box, I will saw you in half."

Tami turned around. A young man with spiky blue hair and a grin on his face smiled at her.

"Do you know how the trick works?" asked Tami.

"Sort of," he said.

"In that case, I will say no thanks. I want to keep all my body parts! I'm

Tami Tripper. Raven Moore hired me to be a museum helper."

"Yes, I heard. My name is Willow. I design the special exhibits."

Tami smiled at Willow. In addition to his blue hair, Willow wore a dark green suit with a dark green shirt and a dark green tie. His sneakers matched his outfit. They were dark green, too. No socks. Willow looked very stylish.

Tami was not stylish. She wore jeans and a T-shirt. Her thick curly hair was hard to control. She usually pulled it into a messy ponytail and forgot about it. Tami looked like her mom with crazy curly hair and large dark eyes. At that moment, Tami's eyes sparkled with amusement.

"Today is my day for meeting people with no socks. I just met Selma Simpson. She wore a lot of clothes, but no socks. Is she okay? I wasn't sure whether to call Hector."

"Oh, Selma is just very old and very forgetful. Her mind wanders. She talks to herself. She meanders through the galleries. She visits Nathan in the basement. She is our museum mascot. We are all fond of Selma."

"Who is Nathan?"

"Nathan Amos is the archivist. Nathan huddles over musty old books and enters information into his computer catalogue. He can tell you the description and location of every item we own." Willow followed Tami into the next gallery, still talking. "Nathan has toiled in the basement for forty years. He is a little old mole, digging, digging, digging into the collection. He scurries around the museum. I don't know what Nathan would do without this place. Some of us have a life away from work."

Tami laughed. "How do you spend your free time?"

"At the theater! That is my first love. The theater is exciting, but the work is not steady. I have a full-time job here. And I love designing the exhibits."

They were in the Tick Tock gallery. Clocks were everywhere. Cuckoo clocks. Grandfather clocks with swinging pendulums. Alarm clocks. Gold clocks. Painted clocks. Everything ticked and tocked. It was noisy!

"Hector winds every clock every

day," said Willow. "He does it when he checks the security cameras." Willow picked up an enameled clock. "Look at this charming clock. It's French. I wish I owned this." Willow sighed and replaced the clock. "Maybe someday, when I win the lottery." He laughed. Willow was a cheerful, fun-loving person. I will enjoy Willow, Tami thought.

"Who else works at the museum?" Tami asked.

"Well, you met Raven Moore. Raven practically lives here. She does the job of three people. She runs the daily oper-ations of the museum. She manages the budget. She deals with the board of directors. She talks to donors. She develops community programs. Raven is dedicated to the museum. We are lucky to have her." Willow paused to admire a Swiss cuckoo clock. "Ritzy Fitzy is another long-time staff member. Maybe longer than Nathan."

"Ritzy Fitzy?"

"Helga Fitzroy. She's the conservator. It is a very important job. She cleans and repairs the collection. She has a laboratory on the top floor. It is filled with oils, cloth, fur, pliers, screwdrivers, saws, brushes. Anything that she might need to repair Sweetie Pie, your favorite duckling. Or a delicate necklace from Gems and Jewels. She is also quite strong from moving heavy items like this grandfather clock. Some small museums have shabby-looking collections. Ours is always clean and everything works."

"Why do you call her Ritzy Fitzy?"

"Oh, that's just my nickname for her. I don't think she likes it though," he added. "Fitzy is very private. Her life is a closed book. She certainly never talks about herself. No one really likes her. But she is an excellent conservator."

"Selma Simpson muttered 'Ritzy Fitzy.'"

"Selma often repeats that rhyme. Helga hates it. She wants Raven to get rid of Selma. She says Selma's mind is failing. Helga wants Nathan gone, too. She thinks Nathan's eyes are too weak to manage the catalogue. Helga pushes Raven to remove Selma and retire Nathan. They argue about it."

"Is there anyone else I should know?" asked Tami.

"You ask a lot of questions. I'm going to call you Ms. Nosy!"

It happened again, thought Tami. Another connection to my mom. "That's what my mom always called me," said Tami. "She also said, 'Mind your own business, Ms. Nosy.'"

"Well, you can ask me as many questions as you like," said Willow. "I love to talk! Right now I am designing a new exhibit for the museum. I call it the Tiny World. Only the smallest items in the collection will be in it. Like this darling clock. Would you like to help me?"

"Of course!"

"I'll talk to Raven and let you know," said Willow.

At home, Tami got out her red clarinet to practice a new song. "Home, Sweet Home" was composed in 1823. "Be it ever so humble, there's no place like home" was Tami's favorite line. It expressed how she felt about her snug apartment. She played the song three times, humming along. Then she packed her favorite lunch for the next day. A peanut butter sandwich and an apple.

Life is good, thought Tami. I love my bike, Ruby. I love my apartment and my mom's paintings. I love my red clarinet. I love my peanut butter sandwiches. I love my new temp job. And Zelda told me there were strange events on the horizon!

CHAPTER 6

PRECIOUS OBJECTS

One morning, Hector was standing in the entrance when Tami arrived. His face was grave.

"Hector. What is wrong? Has something happened?"

"Yes. Please come inside. I have questions for you."

Tami followed Hector to his office. She sat down on a chair. Hector sat behind his desk. He did not smile at Tami. "Hector. You're scaring me! What is going on?"

"Tami, objects have disappeared from the galleries. They may be stolen."

"Do you think I stole them?" Tami

was shocked. "Hector, I would never steal from the Museum of Oddities."

Hector continued. "Have you noticed anything missing when you dust? Little things."

"Can you tell me what is gone?"

"A small crystal ball and a rare deck of tarot cards from Carnival Curiosities."

"I was in that room four days ago. I saw a large crystal ball but not a small one."

"What about the tarot deck?"

"I remember three decks from Italy. Was it one of those?"

"No, it was from Japan." Hector frowned. "We don't know how long it's been gone. Or the crystal ball. It is not valuable, but the blue color was beautiful."

"Anyone could take something small and walk out of the museum," remarked Tami.

"Yes." Hector's expression was grim.

"What can I do?" asked Tami.

"Raven called a meeting for eleven o'clock in the library. Until then, keep your eyes open."

Tami's next dusting job was in Musical Miracles. She searched the displays. Oh no. A dainty Russian music box was missing. She hurried to check the next gallery.

Secrets of the Sea was unique. A replica of a coral reef stretched around three walls. Hundreds of reef inhabitants were represented. Speckled, striped, and solid-colored fish. Sharks, manta rays, an octopus, clams, seahorses, sponges, turtles, crabs, and sea anemones. Tami inspected the exhibit. She spotted a gap near a sea urchin. Something was missing from this gallery, too.

CHAPTER 7

ELEVEN O'CLOCK IN THE LIBRARY

Tami hurried to the museum's library. Dark wood paneling covered the walls. In the center of the room stretched an eight-foot-long table. On the table was an ornate silver tray engraved with the museum's mission: *To Educate, Amaze, and Fascinate the Curious.*

Raven sat at the head of the table. She wore a dark purple dress. Over her shoulders was a cream-colored jacket with a jeweled pin on the lapel. Tami wondered if the pin was from the Gems and Jewels gallery.

Helga Fitzroy sat next to Raven. She

was a tall, thin, unsmiling woman in a drab lab coat. Her back was erect. Her hands were clasped in her lap. She was about sixty years old.

Nathan Amos was a short round man with a pinkish nose. He peered anxiously around the table through thick wire-rimmed glasses. Willow had described Nathan well, thought Tami. He really did look like a mole.

Willow was dressed head to toe in one color again. Today it was gray. His clothes often reflected his mood. Tami realized he was upset.

She took a chair next to Hector. "Relax," he whispered.

Raven opened the meeting. "Precious objects are missing. A small crystal ball and a rare tarot deck are gone from

Carnival Curiosities." Her eyes searched every face.

"Who made the discovery?" asked Nathan.

"Willow. Selecting items for his Tiny World exhibit. Do we know of anything else?"

Tami spoke. "A Russian music box from Musical Miracles."

"A music box?" Nathan turned to Helga. "Weren't you repairing that?"

"I returned that music box to the gallery last week. What are you implying?"

Wow, she is easily insulted, thought Tami.

"And something is missing from Secrets of the Sea, but I don't know what it is," added Tami.

"We have to get to the bottom of

this," said Raven. "We must protect the collection. A thief is at work in our museum."

"Selma drags around a lot of stuffed tote bags." Willow spoke with reluctance.

"I have said it before, and I will say it again, Selma Simpson should not be allowed in this museum. Her mind wanders. She talks nonsense. She pokes around staff rooms. I know she spends too much time with Nathan in the basement. I hear you two chattering away together." Helga glared at Nathan. Her face was frozen in disapproval.

"Selma would never steal from the museum," answered Nathan.

This sounds like a frequent quarrel, thought Tami.

Hector entered the discussion. "I

checked all the cameras. But the stolen items were displayed in corners, out of camera range. Without better security, theft is always possible. Any visitor to the museum could steal the crystal ball, the tarot deck, the music box, and the object from Secrets of the Sea. We have been lucky in the past. We have been lucky so far. Maybe our luck has run out."

"Will I have to cancel my Tiny World exhibit?" wondered Willow.

"No," said Raven. "But the opening must wait until we know more about these thefts." Raven stared at each person in turn. Then she left the room.

"Tami!" Willow pulled her to one side. "I'm so upset! What is happening?" Willow ran his hand through his hair, making it stand on end. "Helga and Nathan are quarreling. Raven suspects we are thieves. Any minute now Hector will start arresting us!"

"Willow, it could be anybody. A visitor. Kids on a school trip. Don't lose heart." Willow was a sensitive, artistic person and easily upset.

Tami went to Hector's office. He had removed his tie and unbuttoned his shirt collar. His suit jacket hung on the back of his chair. His shoulders slumped. "Hector, this is terrible. Can anything be done?"

"We need gallery guards. All museums have them. Even five guards would help."

"Do you suspect someone?" Tami

recalled Willow's comment about the French clock.

Hector frowned at Tami. "That is my concern, not yours."

Well, he told me off, thought Tami. She knew she should not poke her nose into the museum's business. But she was curious.

CHAPTER 8

RITZY FITZY

The next morning, Tami pedaled Ruby to the staff entrance behind the museum. Her thoughts centered on the quarrel between Helga Fitzroy and Nathan Amos. Most of the staff tolerated Selma. Willow called her a museum mascot. Only Helga wanted Selma banned from the building. Tami heard voices. She froze. She did not want anyone to know she was near.

"Ditzy, ritzy, fitzy." Selma chanted nonsense rhymes.

"Stop it, you troublemaker," Helga threatened.

"Down the stairs. Not fair. I remember. I remember," taunted Selma. "Zelda reminded me!"

Tami heard the back door open. Nathan spoke. "Helga, Selma. What's going on?"

"Can I use the bathroom?" asked Selma.

"Go on in," replied Nathan. "Helga, leave Selma alone."

"Nathan, Selma's mind is worse than ever. She chants nonsense rhymes. She is unsteady on her feet. The museum is not a safe place for her. She should be in an institution."

"I will take care of her," responded Nathan.

Helga entered the museum, slamming the door.

What was that all about? Had Zelda's

fortune card unlocked Selma's memory?

Later that morning, Tami climbed the stairs to the top floor of the museum. She was curious about Helga. The door to Helga's lab was at the end of a long hallway. Tami heard Raven and Helga in conversation.

"Helga, please stop harassing me about Selma and Nathan. You are not the head of this museum, I am. Yes, Selma is old and can be annoying. But I don't think she has anyone to take care of her, or anyplace to spend the day. She loves our museum. And that's all I have to say on this subject."

"What about Nathan? His eyes are weak. He should retire."

"That is between Nathan and me. Again, leave it alone, Helga. I know you have work to do. Don't let me keep you from it." Tami dodged into a doorway. She did not want to be caught eavesdropping.

After a few minutes, Tami opened the door to Helga's lab. It was huge. Tami saw animal furs and skins. Bottles of cleaning fluids. Tweezers, scissors, needles, and artist brushes. A tiny hand vacuum. Shelves held pieces waiting to be repaired.

"What are you doing here? This lab is private!" Helga's face was flushed.

"Please excuse me," answered Tami. " I hoped to watch you repair a museum piece."

"Oh alright." Helga picked up an old instrument. "See this lute? The back is slightly cracked. It is delicate work. The sound of the lute could change if I do not repair it well."

"It's fascinating," said Tami. "Did your mother take you to visit museums? Mine did. Is that how you got interested in this work?"

"No she did not. And I do not answer questions about my personal life," Helga's voice was icy. "I suggest you return to your dusting." She turned her back to Tami.

I guess that means I should go! thought Tami. She left the lab. Willow was right. Ritzy Fitzy's life was a closed book. What was she hiding?

CHAPTER 9

NATHAN

Next, Tami walked down to the basement. Stacked in one corner were more of Selma's bags. Nathan was tying one closed. He looked up at Tami's approach.

"Selma is a regular pack rat," commented Tami.

"Yes, she has a collection. Just like the museum," said Nathan.

"Will you show me the computer catalogue?"

"It's not very interesting."

"It is to me," replied Tami. "Your work is critical to the museum. For instance, what is that old book?" Tami pointed to a dusty volume and smiled nicely. She wanted Nathan to like her. Especially after her failure with Ritzy Fitzy.

"This is a ledger from the old days. Archivists, like me, number each object, describe it, and note its location. The number may be hidden underneath, like a chair. Or on a leg tag, like the duckling you named Sweetie Pie. I check that the items are still in our collection and in the correct gallery. My father was the archivist before me, and he did most of this work. But our computer system is more sophisticated. So his work needs to be updated."

"I imagine you spent a lot of time here when you were a boy. The Museum of Oddities is a wonderful place for children."

"Yes, I hope I can keep working here."

"Why would you go?" asked Tami.

"Helga is trying to force me out, because my eyes are bad," said Nathan. "It would break my heart to leave this beautiful collection."

"How will you find the missing piece from Secrets of the Sea?"

"By checking the gallery list."

"I can help you," suggested Tami. "It will go faster."

In the gallery, Tami read from the list while Nathan located each item. Nathan smiled at each piece as he checked its number. Nathan's whole life is this museum, thought Tami. Every piece must seem like it belongs to him.

"Number seventy-two. Exoskeleton of a baby horseshoe crab," Tami read.

Nathan searched the shelves and cabinets. "It's not here. Oh dear, it was very delicate. Only two inches long." He went to notify Raven.

What a shame, thought Tami. Horseshoe crabs are ancient creatures. They have been on earth 445 million years. Why would anyone steal a horseshoe crab?

CHAPTER 10

WHO IS THE THIEF?

Tami biked home slowly that evening. She wondered about the stolen objects. Who was the thief? Was it someone on the museum staff?

At home, Tami sat in her chair and stared at her mom's painting *Enter and Be Amazed*. Had her mom met Sweetie Pie? Or Zelda the fortune teller? What would she tell her mom about the people at the museum?

Raven is friendly when she passes me, but she is so busy that I don't really know her.

Helga's past life is a mystery. I asked one personal question and she got huffy and kicked me out of her lab. Is she hiding the stolen objects?

Nathan roams around the museum. Is he saying goodbye to the special pieces he loves? Or deciding what to steal?

Willow loves that tiny French clock. What other pieces does he covet?

And Hector. Would he stage thefts to force the museum to hire guards?

Poor old Selma has even more bags stored in the basement. Anything could be concealed in those totes.

I hate to think any of them would steal, thought Tami.

CHAPTER 11

BEWARE OF AN OLD MEMORY

Tami was in Gems and Jewels the next morning when Raven entered.

"Is anything else missing?" asked Tami.

"An antique watch from Tick Tock. And I am sorry to tell you that Sweetie Pie is gone, too."

Tami was stunned. Sweetie Pie? Stolen? "Will you call the police?"

"Not yet. I prefer to manage this myself." Raven inspected the shelves and cabinets in Gems and Jewels, then continued to the next gallery, leaving Tami behind.

Sweetie Pie, stolen. Tami was bereft. The duckling was her first love at the Museum of Oddities. Something must be done. I am the museum helper, and the museum needs my help. Maybe I could be a guard, she thought. I'll ask Hector. It is time to stop dusting and start detecting!

Tami climbed the stairs to the third-floor bathroom to store her cleaning supplies. Selma was in the bathroom. Her face was pale and her hands trembled. Tami pulled a chair from the corner and helped Selma to sit. "What is wrong, Selma?"

"It is not a good day for me, dear." Selma smiled sweetly. "Do you work here, dear?"

Uh-oh, thought Tami. Selma usually recognizes me. "Yes, my name is Tamina."

"Tamina means strong. Are you strong?"

"Yes I am." Here was an opportunity to help Selma. "Is there anyone I can call? A relative? A sister or a brother?"

"My sister is dead, dear. Like Hedda's."

"Can you tell me where you are from?"

"From a sad, sad place I want to forget," replied Selma. "Go back to work, Tamina. I will be alright." Selma tried to stand but dropped a tote bag. A small object rolled across the floor. It was the blue crystal ball. "Oh yes. The crystal ball. I am replacing it for Nathan. He is my best friend."

"I will do it for you," said Tami. She felt sad. Perhaps Selma was the thief after all.

Selma seemed recovered, so Tami left her and walked down the three flights of stairs. But just as she reached the first floor, Tami heard a crash, a cry, and a series of loud thuds. Then nothing.

Tami raced back up the stairs. Selma lay on a landing. She had fallen down the stairs from the top floor. Her body was twisted. Her head bled heavily. Tami cradled Selma in her arms. "Help! Help!" she screamed.

Raven ran down from her office. "What happened?"

"Selma fell down the stairs!" cried Tami.

Selma's lips moved. Tami put her

face close. "What is it, Selma?" Tami asked softly.

"*Beware of an old memory*," Selma whispered. Then her eyes rolled back into her head. She was dead.

CHAPTER 12

OLD PEOPLE FALL. IT HAPPENS.

"Oh, oh, oh! Poor Selma!" Tami burst into tears.

Raven took charge. "Tami, go find Hector. Tell him to come quickly. The museum must make a report." She called 911 on her cell phone. "This is Raven Moore at the Museum of Oddities. An elderly visitor fell down a flight of stairs and is dead. Send help immediately."

Hector arrived with Willow. "I'll wait for the police," said Hector. He gently covered Selma with her old moth-eaten coat.

Raven herded Nathan, Willow, and Tami into a nearby room. "Is Helga still in her lab upstairs? She should be here."

Helga showed up but remained silent. Tami continued to weep. Nathan sat stunned. Willow asked, "How did it happen? How did it happen?" over and over.

Finally Helga said, "Willow, stop asking such a stupid question! Selma was frail. She was old. She was confused. She probably had a dizzy spell. She fell down the stairs! It happens! And what about the body?" Helga was indignant. "It can't be left here. The museum has to open to the public."

"We must wait for the police," said Nathan. "Then we can decide what should be done."

"Maybe a funeral," suggested Willow.

"That's ridiculous," sputtered Helga.

"Selma was a stranger to us. We are not responsible."

Helga does not care that Selma is dead, thought Tami. She wanted Selma out of the museum, and now her wish has come true. What a hard-hearted woman.

"I will take care of everything." Nathan's voice silenced Helga.

The rest of the day passed in a blur. Raven and Hector met with the police. Helga remained shut up in her lab. Willow wandered around mournfully, selecting pieces for his Tiny World exhibit. Tami sat with Nathan in the basement.

"What did Selma say to you?" asked Nathan.

"*Beware of an old memory.* Does that mean anything to you?"

"Possibly," replied Nathan. His eyes were sorrowful. "I think I will go home. I don't want to be here."

Tami found Hector in his office. "What did the police say?" she asked.

"They examined Selma's body and walked up and down the staircase. We explained who she was. It was clear to everyone that it was a sad accident. An old lady, unsteady on her feet, tumbled down the stairs."

"Oh, *why* didn't I stay with her? It's my fault!"

"Tami, you couldn't know it would happen."

"Look." Tami handed Hector the

small blue crystal ball. "This fell out of Selma's tote bag."

Hector gently placed the crystal ball on his desk. "Selma was the thief after all. What a shame. Maybe her mind was worse than we thought."

"She said Nathan wanted her to replace it. Do you think Nathan knew Selma was taking things, and he didn't tell you?"

"I hope not. We will have to go through Selma's tote bags thoroughly." Hector sighed. "It can wait until tomorrow. Why don't you go home? We have closed the museum."

CHAPTER 13

"CLAIR DE LUNE"

Tami biked home on Ruby. What an awful situation! Poor Selma was frail and confused, but she should not have tumbled down the stairs. Why didn't I stay with her, mourned Tami. She felt so guilty.

In her apartment, Tami went to the bathroom and splashed cold water on her face. She gazed into the mirror. Her eyes were puffy from her tears. Usually they had a twinkle. But at the moment, her dark eyes were thoughtful.

Tami went to her window and gazed out. Stars studded a purple evening sky. I need comforting, she thought. She picked up her clarinet and played "Clair de Lune" by Claude Debussy. "Clair de Lune" means "moonlight." It is soft, slow, dreamy music, and it helped Tami feel better. She only played half of the piece because the rest was very difficult. But she practiced it often. I do not give up, thought Tami. Tamina means strong.

Tami continued to worry about Selma's dying words. Was Selma telling me something? What was the old memory? And *who* was Hedda?

CHAPTER 14

MS. NOSY

The following morning Tami went straight to the basement. She wanted to examine the tote bags before anyone else. She dumped out the contents of one tote. Two sweaters with holes in them. A pair of sweatpants. Two men's shirts. A long cotton skirt. A knitted cap. A pair of mittens. A blanket. Unopened mail addressed to a post office mailbox. Tami continued to empty the bag. A knife, fork, and spoon. A can opener. A plastic cup and plate. A box of matches. Was Selma sleeping in the park? Again, Tami felt guilty about Selma's fall down the stairs.

Tami opened the second bag. At last, Selma's private box. She lifted the lid. Inside was a creased black-and-white photo of a family dressed for summer. A father, a mother, a young girl, and a baby. *Pinetree Falls August 1952* was written on the photo. She found a faded birth announcement. Selma was born in 1940. She had been eighty-three years old. Tami's eyes filled with tears. This was so sad! Two yellowed newspaper articles were folded up in the very bottom of the box.

Tragedy in Pinetree Falls. Fire Kills Three Family Members.
Daughter Orphaned by Blaze.

Below the headline was a photo of a burning house. In front, a firefighter held the hand of a young girl. Tami peered at the picture. Was it Selma? What happened to that young girl? Where did she go? Tami went to the next article.

Doors Close at Pinetree County Children's Home

Once, the Children's Home sheltered hundreds of children. Many were orphans or had families that could not care for them. Others came through the court system. These days, most children are placed in foster care. After one hundred years, Pinetree County Children's Home has closed its doors forever.

Tami read the article twice. Was this Selma's "sad, sad place"? She tucked the private box into her backpack. Tami knew her mom would say, "Mind your own business, Ms. Nosy." I'll give this to Hector, Tami promised herself.

But not today.

CHAPTER 15

WHAT DOES NATHAN KNOW?

Tami delved into a third tote bag. More unopened mail. A few old newspapers. An old spiral notebook. A child's jump rope. A faded woman's glove. A man's handkerchief. And a tiny jewelry box. In it was the exoskeleton of a baby horseshoe crab.

Uh-oh, thought Tami.

Just then, Hector arrived. "Have you found anything?"

"She had a post office box. And some unopened mail."

"I will follow that up," said Hector. "What else?"

"An assortment of clothes and

personal items. And an old glove, a man's handkerchief, a jump rope, and an old notebook."

At that moment, Nathan entered the basement workroom. His shoulders drooped. His feet dragged. He sat at his worktable and dropped his head into his hands. Nathan has aged overnight, thought Tami.

Hector told Nathan what Tami found in the tote bags.

Nathan did not look up. "I know about that stuff."

"Selma also had this," said Tami. She showed them the tiny horseshoe crab.

"Nathan, did you know about this horseshoe crab? Or about the blue crystal ball? Selma had that, too." Hector was furious.

Nathan shifted uneasily in his chair. "No."

He's lying, thought Tami. Why?

Hector studied Nathan in silence. Tami remembered that Hector was a retired police detective. He would not stop until he got all the answers. They left the basement together.

"Hector, I was going to ask you if I could be a security guard."

"You know what? That's a good idea. We need to increase our security, and I appreciate all the help I can get."

"Thank you!" Tami was delighted. She could still enjoy the museum, but she would not have to dust anything.

It was a busy day. Two groups of schoolchildren toured the museum. Tami roamed through the galleries.

Who knew where Selma hid the tarot decks, the music box, the antique watch, or Sweetie Pie?

Gems and Jewels was a small gallery tucked at the back of the museum. Not many people found it. Just as she was about to enter, Tami heard Helga's voice.

"Maybe Selma wasn't the thief, Nathan. Maybe it was someone else. If I'm right, you may have to retire sooner than you want."

"Don't assume too much, Ritzy Fitzy. Selma had a notebook. Raven might find it interesting reading."

Tami was spellbound. What was this all about? Did Nathan have the old spiral notebook?

"You wouldn't dare," hissed Helga.

"I will if I have to, Ritzy Fitzy."

"Don't call me that!"

"Then stop threatening me!" Nathan stormed out, passing Tami. Helga remained inside. The room was silent. Tami heard an angry sob. I better get out of here, she thought.

At home, Tami puzzled over the conversation she heard. Helga wanted Nathan out. Why? What was she so afraid of? I need to know more about Helga's hidden past, thought Tami.

Tami knew quite a bit about the other staff members. Raven was forty-two years old. She had earned a top degree from an elite university. She attended conferences. She gave speeches. Raven was a well-known person in the museum world.

Hector was about fifty. He joined the museum after an illustrious career with the police. He was a decorated police officer with a spotless record. Awards hung on his office walls.

Willow was a chatty, friendly man. Before coming to the museum, Willow was an assistant set designer at a local theater. He regaled Tami with stories about the theater people he knew. They often lunched together in the park across the street. Last week they celebrated Willow's thirtieth birthday with a cupcake. There was nothing mysterious about Willow.

Nathan was quiet and shy. But Tami

knew about Nathan, too. His childhood roaming the museum while his father worked. His tidy apartment nearby. His mixed-breed dog, Oddie, named after the museum. Nathan was sixty years old, and the Museum of Oddities was his home.

But what about Helga? That closed book frustrated Tami.

And poor old Selma. Was Pinetree Falls the key to her story?

Finally, *where was Sweetie Pie?*

CHAPTER 16

TAMI TAKES A DAY OFF

"It is okay to miss a day of work, Tami," said Raven. "Is everything alright?"

"Of course." Tami felt guilty about not giving a reason for her request. I should hand over Selma's box, Tami thought. But not yet.

Tami attached bicycle saddlebags to Ruby. Pinetree Falls was about three hours away, so she prepared for the trip. She loaded up on peanut butter sandwiches and apples. Also M&M's, her favorite candy. Plenty of water. A rain poncho just in case. Sunscreen. A battery to charge her phone. And her bike repair kit. Just before hopping onto

Ruby, Tami pulled her curly hair into a ponytail and put on her helmet. She did not want her hair blowing around her face as she rode. It was annoying.

The day was bright and cool. Perfect for distance riding. As Tami pedaled along on Ruby, she thought about the relationship between Selma and Nathan. Selma frequently said, "Nathan is my best friend." What had Selma told Nathan? Tami was sure Nathan had lied about the thefts. There is more to that story, thought Tami as she arrived at Pinetree Falls.

It was a pretty town. Tami saw a park with a duck pond and a playground. There was a café and a drugstore. A bank. An elementary school. And a grocery store. People were going about their business. Tami found the newspaper office at the end of the street.

"I'm interested in newspapers from 1952." Tami spoke to a young man working at a computer. He looked up at her voice.

"That's a long time ago," he said. "We don't keep them here. They are on microfilm at the library. It's on the next block."

If you are a curious person, like Tami, libraries are a source of information and entertainment. Tami loved to visit them. A children's section had low bookshelves and beanbag chairs where kids could read. Another corner had computers for library visitors. Rows and rows of standing shelves held the library's book collection. Tami approached a smiling, gray-haired woman at the librarian's desk.

"I'm doing some research and need old newspaper files from 1952. Can you help me?"

"I would be delighted. What are you looking for?"

"I'm curious about this photo. I suspect I know who this child was." Tami showed the librarian the photo of the young girl in front of the burned house.

"What a terrible event. Let's see. 1952 is a long time ago. It will be on microfilm."

Microfilm is stored on reels threaded through a machine that looks like an old computer. Tami turned the viewer handle slowly and scanned the screen until she found the article.

Tragedy in Pinetree Falls. Fire kills three family members. Young daughter orphaned by blaze. Yesterday, November 5, Brenda and Robert Simpson and their infant daughter died in a fire that engulfed their home. Fire officials believe that faulty electrical wiring was the cause. Firefighters rushed to the scene but were unable to stop the blaze or rescue the victims. Twelve-year-old Selma was at a music lesson at the time. She arrived home to discover the tragedy.

I was right, thought Tami. The young girl was Selma. What a tragic story. She returned to the librarian. "I am also interested in the history of the Pinetree County Children's Home."

"I remember when it closed," said the

woman. "People lost their jobs. I think it was in 2000. Those records are at the county courthouse. Did you have a family member at the children's home?"

"No. But I think the young girl in the photo was sent there. Selma Simpson. I am interested in her story."

"Are you a journalist or a writer?"

"No. Just a very, very, very curious person."

CHAPTER 17

WHO WAS HEDDA?

Like everything in Pinetree Falls, the county courthouse was not far away.

"Hi, I hope you can help me. I am researching the history of the Pinetree County Children's Home." Tami smiled at the clerk behind the desk.

He smiled back. "The records are stored in boxes. It is a lot of musty old files."

Tami followed the young man to a storage room. The boxes were stacked on metal shelves. She found a file folder with names of the children who lived at the home. She quickly found *Selma*

Simpson, November 1952–1958. File S201.

File S201 described Selma's life at the county home. She was a friendly child who became a warm, outgoing young woman. She helped with the younger kids. At age eighteen Selma was too old to remain. She got a college degree, returned to the home, and became a teacher, "responsible for Hedda D."

Hedda! That name again. Tami went back to the list of children. She found *Hedda Ditz, 1970–1980. File D15.*

File D15 was thick. Hedda Ditz arrived when she was eight years old. She was sent by the county justice system. Tami found official court papers, but most of the information was blacked out. She read Selma's notes about Hedda. Hedda was an angry little girl with a dark past. The children teased her with a cruel jump rope song. As she got older, Hedda's anger turned inward. She became silent and aloof. Hedda remained at the home until she was eighteen. Then she disappeared.

Tami mulled over this strange history. When the Pinetree County Children's Home closed, Selma was sixty years old. Twenty years later she appeared at the museum, a confused old woman, dragging her life around in tote bags.

It was time to go back. Tami made copies of the file. When she bent to pick up her backpack, she found a piece of paper on the floor. It was a recent newspaper article.

Pinetree County Children's Home has been closed for many years, but some things remain. Pinetree Falls girls still chant this jump rope rhyme.

Hedda Ditz, rhymes with ritz.
On a Monday had a fit.
Pushed her sister down the stairs.
It really wasn't very fair!
One, two, three, four, five . . .

Tami was stunned. She grabbed her stuff and ran out of the library. Soon she was pedaling as fast as she could on Ruby back to the museum.

CHAPTER 18

ANOTHER *FALL?*

At the museum, Willow rushed up to her. "Tami, thank goodness you are back! Nathan had a fall! He's in the hospital!"

Another fall? "What happened?"

"No one knows. Hector found Nathan unconscious in the parking lot. Maybe he had a stroke. The hospital ordered a brain scan. It's one bad thing after another!" Willow was almost in tears.

Tami went straight to Raven's office. "I'll go to the hospital," she told Raven.

"Oh thank you!" Raven sighed. "I'm a capable woman, Tami, but events are really testing me. Can you go right now? Hector is there, but I need him." She looked exhausted.

"Don't worry about a thing. I will find out how Nathan is. I know a lot of the doctors there." Tami spent many hours at the hospital when her mom had cancer.

Tami stopped by the basement to pick up a few things for Nathan. She chose the framed picture of his sweet old dog, Oddie. She opened Nathan's backpack to put the photo inside. To her dismay, the first thing she saw was the Russian music box. Underneath was the antique watch. Then the tarot deck. Including the blue crystal ball and the horseshoe crab, only one more item was missing. Tami dug all the way to the bottom of the backpack. But Sweetie Pie was not there.

Tami knew she should give the backpack to Raven. But she thought Nathan had a right to explain first. Again, Tami decided to wait. She left the backpack, but took Oddie's picture. She hopped on Ruby and pedaled to the hospital.

CHAPTER 19

NATHAN EXPLAINS

Tami sat down next to Hector. Nathan's eyes were closed and he breathed normally, but he was very banged up.

"I opened Selma's mail," remarked Hector. "Most of it was from this very hospital. Selma had dementia. That's why she was confused. She couldn't remember anything."

"Hector, Selma did recover one memory. She said to Helga, 'I remember. I remember. Zelda reminded me.'" Tami paused. Should she tell more?

"I guess we will never know what it was," sighed Hector. "Well, Raven is waiting for me." He walked slowly out of the hospital room.

An hour later, Nathan's doctor entered. "Hi Tami. How have you been? Nathan's brain scan is clear. No stroke. It was a serious fall and a nasty knock on the head, but he is alright. He should be conscious anytime now."

"That's wonderful news. His friends at the museum will be so relieved."

The doctor left. Tami opened a book and prepared to wait. She was reminded of the many days and nights she sat with her mom. That was a long, sad time for the two of them. Tami's mom said, "I do not worry about you, Tami. You are strong like your name, Tamina. You will be alright."

My mom was right, thought Tami. I miss her, but I am okay.

Just then, Nathan stirred. His eyes opened. He looked around the room.

"You are in the hospital, Nathan. Hector found you in the parking lot. You were unconscious. But don't worry. The doctor said you are okay." She handed him Oddie's photo. "I was going to bring your backpack, but I decided to leave it."

"Did you look inside?"

"Yes."

Nathan sighed. "I was going to tell Raven. Everyone thought Selma was the thief. That wasn't fair. She was innocent."

"Why did you take those things?"

"Oh, I was so unhappy. Helga was forcing me out. I wanted a little collection of my own."

"Did Selma know?"

"I suppose so. She found the crystal ball and the horseshoe crab. She planned to return them so no one would know it was me. Selma was a loyal friend. After she fell, I found her spiral notebook. It didn't make much sense because of her dementia. But she obviously knew some terrible secret about Helga. I pretended to know what it was, and I threatened Helga with exposure. I wanted her to leave me alone." Nathan frowned.

"I fell in the parking lot on my way home. I must have tripped over something I didn't see. Maybe my eyes are worse. Now Raven will ask me to retire after all. I will miss my beloved museum." Nathan's lips trembled.

"I don't think you fell, Nathan. I think you were pushed very, very hard by a very frightened person. And so was Selma. Nathan, I have to get back to the museum. I will explain everything later."

CHAPTER 20

ZELDA'S FORTUNE

Tami found Helga in Raven's office. "I told you so," Helga was saying. "Nathan's eyes are bad. That is why he fell. He needs to retire!"

"Let's not be hasty," replied Raven. "We can wait until Nathan leaves the hospital to decide anything."

Helga noticed Tami standing in the doorway. "What are you doing here?"

"I've seen Nathan," answered Tami. "He's fine. No stroke."

"I suppose he fell, like Selma," sighed Raven.

"That's what I would like to talk

about," said Tami. "Will you ask Hector and Willow to join us?"

When Raven, Hector, Willow, and Helga were seated in Raven's office, Tami began. "I first met Selma in Carnival Curiosities. We got our fortunes told. When Zelda said *Beware of an old memory*, Selma was startled. She whispered 'Ritzy Fitzy,' and wondered, 'Is it my lost memory?' She was upset and confused.

"The day she died Selma told me she was from a 'sad, sad place.' She told me her sister was dead, 'like Hedda's.' I was concerned about her. But she said she was alright. So I left her. Suddenly there was a crash and a cry. Selma had fallen down a long flight of stairs from the third floor. I held her in my arms. As she died, she whispered *Beware of an old memory.*

"I felt so guilty about Selma's fall. And I wanted to learn more about her. So the next morning I searched her tote bags for Selma's private box." Tami placed the contents on Raven's desk. "I wanted to know if Selma was the girl in this photo. I rode Ruby to Pinetree Falls. I read old newspaper files and examined records from the Pinetree County Children's Home. I learned a lot."

Tension filled the room. Willow wiggled in his chair with excitement. Raven did not take her eyes off Tami. Hector frowned in concentration. Only Helga betrayed anxiety. Her face was pale. Her hands were clenched in her lap. Her eyes darted from person to person.

Tami continued. "Selma lived at the children's home after a fire killed her family. She stayed for forty-eight years. She became a teacher and was responsible for a girl named Hedda Ditz." Tami laid the jump rope cartoon on the desk.

"*Hedda Ditz, rhymes with ritz, on a Monday had a fit*," read Raven.

Hector jumped to his feet. "Ditz ritz fitz! Ritzy Fitzy!" He pointed at Helga. "*You* are Hedda Ditz! The child who pushed her sister down the stairs!"

"That is ridiculous!" said Helga. "My name is Helga Fitzroy!"

"You changed your name to hide your past," said Tami. "You became a museum conservator. You thought you were safe here. It must have been a shock when Selma turned up. But you were lucky. Selma had dementia. Then one day, Selma's memory returned. She told you, 'I remember. I remember.' So Selma had to go."

"No! No! Selma was confused!" Helga jumped to her feet. Her eyes were on the door.

Hector grabbed Helga's arm. He picked up the telephone. "I'm calling the police!"

Helga yanked her arm away and ran down the hall to her lab. She slammed the door and turned the key. Hector raced after her. He yelled through the door. "Helga! You pushed Selma down the stairs! And pushed Nathan, too! Just like you pushed your little sister!"

Helga let out a frightening shriek. "Yes! I pushed her! She was a little pest! It made me mad! And I pushed Selma and Nathan! They were going to tell!" She beat the door with her fists. She smashed equipment. At last the police arrived and removed a struggling, screaming Helga.

Raven, Hector, Willow, and Tami collapsed in Raven's office. It was hard to believe that the frantic woman taken away by the police was the icy, aloof Helga.

Willow wondered, "Was it all because I called her Ritzy Fitzy, and Selma heard me?" Then his face fell. "Poor Selma. Was her death my fault?"

"No," said Raven. "Selma might have remembered anyway." She jumped up. "Let's go to the hospital. I want to tell Nathan he will always have a job at the Museum of Oddities."

CHAPTER 21

TIME TO SAY GOODBYE

The Museum of Oddities was back to normal. Nathan was forgiven. Raven interviewed candidates to replace Helga. Hector patrolled the galleries with his new team of security guards. Willow's Tiny World was ready to open. Hundreds of beautiful little objects were arranged throughout the museum. A large poster beckoned visitors to enter.

Welcome to the Tiny World
An exhibit to educate, amaze,
and fascinate the curious

The staff gathered to celebrate the exhibit opening. Willow's clothes reflected his excitement. He wore a bright blue shirt, slacks, jacket, and sneakers to match his spiky blue hair.

"All Helga had to do was tell me," said Raven. "She was a wonderful conservator. We could have worked it out."

"She lived her life in fear of discovery," said Nathan. "She must have felt constantly under threat. And when Selma appeared Helga panicked."

"So she started her campaign to get rid of Selma," said Hector.

"And me," added Nathan. "She was frightened by my friendship with Selma."

"But Tami stopped her!" Willow gave Tami an enormous hug. Then his face fell. "Why do you have to leave, Tami? We love you. And we are grateful to you!"

"When Zelda told me *Strange events are on the horizon*, I never suspected she meant murder. Poor Selma! I will miss her. And I will miss all of you. But I think my job as a museum helper has come to an end," replied Tami. "There is only one thing I am unhappy about."

"What is that?" asked Raven.

"Sweetie Pie!"

Everybody laughed.

"It's not funny," protested Tami.

"Maybe this will ease the pain." Raven handed Tami a package tied with a ruby-red ribbon. "It is a gift of thanks from the Museum of Oddities."

"And from me," added Nathan with a guilty smile. "There was one more tote bag."

Inside the package was an adorable

two-headed duckling. It was tiny and fluffy and had a sweet expression. Both little heads smiled at Tami. Her eyes filled with tears.

"Oh thank you! I will treasure this gift forever. But it is time for me to go." She hugged everyone, walked down the stairs to the lobby, and went out the entrance doors.

Tami paused on the steps of the Museum of Oddities. She gazed at the blue archway with its exotic creatures. She thought about her mom and the painting titled *Enter and Be Amazed.*

We still share things, thought Tami. With a smile, she hopped on Ruby and pedaled home.

9 781956 476279